Ears

Written by Carol Krueger

Rigby

Look at the elephants.
Look at their big ears.
The ears can help
the elephants stay cool.

This hippo has ears
on the top of its head.
When the hippo
is in the water,
its ears can stay out.

This fox has big ears.
Its ears can hear insects.
They help the fox
get insects to eat.

Polar bears have
small ears.
They have fur on their ears.
When it is cold,
the fur helps the ears
stay warm.

fur

This camel lives
in the desert.
It has hair in its ears.
Sand will not
get in its ears.

This insect has
no ears on its head.
The ears are on
its knees.

knee
ear

This crocodile
has ears by its eyes.
It can shut its ears
under the water.
The water can't get
into its ears.

Index

Guide Notes

Title: Ears
Stage: Early (3) – Blue

Genre: Nonfiction
Approach: Guided Reading
Processes: Thinking Critically, Exploring Language, Processing Information
Written and Visual Focus: Photographs (static images), Index, Labels

THINKING CRITICALLY

(sample questions)

- Look at the front cover and the title. Ask the children what they know about animals' ears.
- Look at the title and read it to the children.
- Focus the children's attention on the index. Ask: "What are you going to find out about in this book?"
- If you want to find out about big ears, which pages would you look on?
- If you want to find out about ears with fur, which page would you look on?
- Look at pages 12 and 13. Why do you think an insect has ears on its knees?
- How do you think an elephant uses its ears to stay cool?

EXPLORING LANGUAGE

Terminology

Title, cover, photographs, author, photographers

Vocabulary

Interest words: elephants, hippo, camel, insects, desert, knees, crocodile
High-frequency words: helps, when, their, eat
Positional words: on, under, in, out, into

Print Conventions

Capital letter for sentence beginnings, periods, commas